THE BOOM ROOM

RICK BLECHTA

RAVEN BOOKS
an imprint of
ORCA BOOK PUBLISHERS

Blechta, Rick, author
The boom room / Rick Blechta.
(Rapid reads)

Issued in print and electronic formats.
ISBN 978-1-4598-0514-9 (pbk.).--ISBN 978-1-4598-0515-6 (pdf).--
ISBN 978-1-4598-0516-3 (epub)

I. Title. II. Series: Rapid reads
PS8553.L3969B65 2014   c813'.54   C2013-907630-1
C2013-907631-X

First published in the United States, 2014
Library of Congress Control Number: 2013956421

Summary: When the prime suspect in a nightclub murder turns out to be
his partner's half brother, Detective Mervin Pratt soon realizes that the case
is not quite so open-and-shut as it first appears. (RL 4.2)

*Orca Book Publishers is dedicated to preserving the environment and has
printed this book on Forest Stewardship Council® certified paper.*

Orca Book Publishers gratefully acknowledges the support for
its publishing programs provided by the following agencies:
the Government of Canada through the Canada Book Fund and the
Canada Council for the Arts, and the Province of British Columbia
through the BC Arts Council and the Book Publishing Tax Credit.

Design by Jenn Playford
Cover photography by plainpicture

ORCA BOOK PUBLISHERS
PO Box 5626, Stn. B
Victoria, BC Canada
V8R 6S4

ORCA BOOK PUBLISHERS
PO Box 468
Custer, WA USA
98240-0468

www.orcabook.com
Printed and bound in Canada.

17 16 15 14 • 4 3 2 1

This one is dedicated to Ted Blechta
for no other reason than
you're the greatest brother
in the world.

CHAPTER ONE

Pratt was digging into a nice plate of pasta at his favorite Italian restaurant. He knew he shouldn't eat the stuff. But so what if a few extra pounds showed on his six-foot frame? He deserved a treat now and then.

He was about to shovel in his third mouthful when he got the call.

"We need help at a crime scene," dispatch told him.

The detective looked at his cell phone like it was a traitor. Why couldn't they have called him last night, when he'd just gone home after work?

With a sigh, he put the phone back to his ear. "Where?"

"Nightclub district. A stiff's turned up stabbed at The Boom Room. Heard of it?"

"Yes, but not in a way that makes me eager to visit."

"We sent Snow and Gordon down, but Snow has pulled up lame. Gordon is alone and could use help."

"Why me?" Pratt asked. Everyone knew there was bad blood between Gordon and him.

"You're the closest to the crime scene."

"How do you know that?"

The dispatcher chuckled. "We have our ways."

"You rat!"

"Hey, Pratt, I'm just doing my job. Just get a doggie bag for your dinner."

Signaling for the waiter, Pratt sighed again. "I'll be there ASAP."

* * *

It was true he wasn't far away. But it was Friday, and traffic was impossible. Kids were flooding downtown on this late-winter evening. Pratt could have walked there faster. Even with the magnetic bubblegum light on top of his car, no one gave him an inch.

Finally driving up to the yellow police tape, he got out. The patrolman on duty almost said something, but Pratt's glare shut him up. His cell phone rang again.

"Pratt here. What do you want?"

The person at the other end laughed. "Boy, are you in a crabby mood!"

It was Ellis, his still-wet-behind-the-ears partner. The lad had good "cop instincts," so Pratt had taken him on. Two months later, the fit was still good. He didn't make Pratt always feel like the old fart on the homicide squad.

"What do you want?"

"I hear you got called in to help Gordon," the younger man said.

"Bad news travels fast."

"Want some company? I have nothing on tonight."

"Suit yourself. You know how Gordon can be."

"That's why I'm offering."

"Well, in that case, sure. You might learn something about how not to interact with the public."

"See you in half an hour."

"The traffic is horrible," Pratt warned him.

"It always is down there on Fridays. I'm taking transit."

Police tape extended across the street from both corners of the building housing The Boom Room. A large crowd pressed forward against the flimsy plastic strips. Four uniformed cops kept it back.

The Boom Room stank of stale beer and sweat. Two distinct groups crowded around a couple of tables at the back of the long room, looking uneasily at each other. Two more uniformed cops stood nearby, keeping an eye on them. Pratt also noticed three girls sitting in a corner by themselves. One was sobbing uncontrollably. The other two were comforting her.

The club must have been packed when the murder was discovered. Where the hell were all those people? Why hadn't Gordon made some attempt to keep them there?

Pratt knew one of the uniforms and went up to him. "Where's Gordon?"

The cop motioned with his head.

"In the basement. Manager's office. Crime scene guys are down there too. I have no idea what's going on, so don't ask."

Pratt headed for the door the cop had pointed to. Passing the club's small kitchen, he saw a uniform talking with the three-man cooking crew.

Sticking his head in, he asked, "Taking statements?"

This cop turned and rolled his eyes.

"Something like that. Speaking English is not their strong point."

"Gordon?"

"Downstairs. Stairway's at the end of the corridor on the right."

Back here, the reek of old cooking oil was added to the stench of beer. The steps to the basement were sticky and slimy at the same time. Pratt gripped the railing tightly.

At the bottom he found a small square room. Painted flat black some years ago, it was now a dusty dark gray. A door on the left stood open. Two white-suited crime techs were in there. Pratt could clearly see the body slumped over a desk. There wasn't as much blood as he'd expected with a stabbing.

He didn't need to ask where Gordon was. His loud voice could be heard behind a door marked *Employees Only*.

Gordon looked up as Pratt entered. His face wasn't friendly, but then, it seldom was when Pratt was around.

The space was a locker room for employees and doubled as the dressing room for bands. Everything was low-rent and dirty: lockers, a few chairs, a table, a cheap metal coatrack. The full-length mirror on the back wall had a big crack through it. On a chair in front of it huddled a scared-looking twenty-something kid. Gordon motioned Pratt out of the room. He followed and shut the door.

"Do you think it's wise leaving your suspect alone?" Pratt asked.

Gordon ignored him.

"So you got sent?"

Pratt nodded. "How come Snow isn't here?"

"He got sick earlier this evening. Says he has the flu. It's bullshit. He wanted a head start on his weekend. Well, the joke's on him. You too, for that matter. This is an open-and-shut case."

"That kid in the room?"

"Guilty as sin. I was about to take him downtown."

Pratt raised his eyebrows. "He's confessed?"

"Get real, Pratt. They all say they're innocent. Here are the facts. The kid is the leader of the band playing here tonight. He had a screaming argument with Lewis, the owner, this afternoon when they were setting up. Everybody saw it. Then he went around telling everyone what a scumbag the guy was. Said he was going to get him. The club manager heard him. A few hours later, someone sticks a knife in Lewis's back. And guess who was always flashing a knife—including earlier this evening? The one he claims has now gone missing."

"That's pretty compelling."

"Damn straight it is! I had to laugh when the kid said he didn't do it."

"And what if he's telling you the truth?"

Gordon stepped right into Pratt's face.

"Know what your problem is, Pratt? You think you're smarter than everyone else. Well, you're not, and I'm going to prove it.

A couple hours' grilling downtown and this kid will fold like a cheap suitcase. You'll see."

As Gordon went back into the room, Pratt was thinking it was a good thing they had CCTV in the interview rooms now. In the bad old days, cops like Gordon would have beaten a confession out of the kid.

He sighed. Seldom was a case this easy. The problem wasn't that he thought he was smarter than anybody. The problem was Gordon's lack of imagination—and his laziness. If the kid got a good attorney, Gordon's case could wind up shredded. It did look bad for the suspect, but every aspect of a case should be carefully studied. That was the only proper way to investigate a murder.

He sometimes wished he could take the easy way out—like Gordon.

But then, he knew, he wouldn't be doing his job.

CHAPTER TWO

Pratt moved back to the doorway of the crime scene room. Two techs in their white "bunny suits" were busy working it up. He knew better than to enter.

"Have a minute, guys?"

The one closest to the door took a few more photos of the body before turning.

"Sure, Pratt. What can I do for you?"

That was unexpected. Usually, they told detectives to bugger off and let them work.

"Anything interesting to report?"

The tech shrugged.

"Pretty simple. The doc hasn't arrived yet, but it looks like the late Joseph Lewis met his end from one stab wound in the left side of his back. Right into the heart. The death wound was made by a knife with a thin blade. Sharpened on both sides, probably with a long blade."

"Switch blade? Stiletto?"

The tech nodded.

"Death would have been very quick. You can see there's not much blood."

"Any sign of the murder weapon?"

"You can see the room is a pigsty. My guess is we won't find the murder weapon in here, but we have to look anyway, don't we?"

"Let us know if anything interesting comes to light. Okay? Looks like I'm going to be upstairs for a few hours."

"Sure."

Things had to be done the right way or the case could fall apart in court in a big hurry. With Gordon so focused on his suspect, Pratt knew he wasn't paying attention to much else. Since Snow was down for the count, at least for tonight, it was up to Pratt to attend to the important details.

Someone else was clumping down the stairs. It was past time to post a person at the top to keep people away from the crime scene.

Pratt turned to see his young partner, Ellis. Tall, dark-haired and decidedly handsome, he was dressed casually, but his eyes were busy, anything but off duty.

"You got here quickly."

"I was already downtown for the evening," Ellis answered, but there was something odd about the tone of his voice.

"Why did you offer to come in on this?"

"I know what this place is like on a Friday night. I figured you'd have your hands full."

"You've been here before?"

"Yeah. A few times."

Again, the feeling something wasn't quite right.

Ellis continued. "Where's the suspect?"

At that moment, the door to the dressing room opened. Gordon frog-marched his handcuffed murder suspect in front of him.

"What are you doing here?" he asked Ellis. "Should have expected that when I got Frick, Frack wouldn't be far behind."

"I thought you could use some help. This club must have been full of people when the shit hit the fan. If you don't want help, I'll just leave."

"Suit yourself, Cubby," Gordon shot back as he pushed his suspect toward the stairs.

Pratt hadn't said a word, but he was certain something had flashed between the suspect and Ellis as he'd passed by. Eyes never lied if you knew what to watch for—and when.

"We need to talk," he told Ellis, leading him into the empty dressing room. "What's going on?"

"I came down to help."

"Did you? That's the only reason?"

Ellis looked as if he might try to brazen it out. He started to speak twice, then deflated and sat down on one of the folding chairs.

"The kid Gordon is fingering for the murder…"

"Yeah. What about him?"

"He's my half brother."

CHAPTER THREE

P ratt could remember only three other times he had been rendered totally speechless. The last was when his wife had walked out on him three years earlier.

Ellis sighed heavily.

"I haven't told you, but my dad was killed when I was five. Car accident. My mom remarried three years later, and the kid you just met was the result. Jamie Clark is my half brother. We haven't had any contact in nearly five years."

"Reason?"

"Well…let's just say he didn't see eye to eye with the rest of the family. One night we'd all had enough and my stepdad asked him to leave."

Pratt raised an eyebrow.

"Asked?"

"Okay. He booted Jamie's ass out the door. Satisfied?"

"Has anyone in the family had contact with him since?"

Another sigh.

"Obviously, my mother did. She was the one who told me Jamie was in trouble down here tonight. He always was her little darling."

"You sound jealous."

"Oddly, I think he was jealous of me, or at least envious."

"Why?"

Ellis finally looked up at Pratt.

"Because I was always 'the good son.' No matter what Jamie did, it was never good enough in my stepdad's eyes. Yeah, he was a wild kid. Didn't care about school. But there were good things about him that never seemed to count for much. His music, for instance."

"When was the last time you saw or spoke to him?"

"The night he left. I was starting with the force and thought I knew it all."

"Then someone gave your mom the news about what happened tonight. Who was that?"

"I didn't think to ask."

Pratt wasn't satisfied with that answer but filed it away for later.

"So your mother told you about this mess and you thought it would be okay to come down here to check it all out?" He made sure he had his partner's full attention. "Are you actually that stupid?"

"I didn't stop to think. Mom was really upset."

"Shall I lay out what you've probably done? Compromised this case, is all. We might not be able to take it to court because of what you've done."

"I had to do something."

"You want to do something? Use your brain. Get up!"

"Why?"

"Because I'm booting your ass out the door in order to try to save it. If they get wind of this downtown, you're toast. Understand?"

They went back upstairs, where Pratt loudly sent Ellis on his way, saying it was his night off and to go out and enjoy it. He hoped the other cops bought it. When Ellis's relationship to the suspect got out— and it would sooner or later—he wanted everyone present to remember Ellis being on the scene for only a few minutes.

At the door to the club, he leaned over and whispered, "Now get out and pray to God no one finds out you're the suspect's damn brother."

Ellis pursed his lips.

"Sorry I let you down. I didn't know what else to do."

Pratt clapped his partner on the back. "Just leave, okay?"

* * *

It was a long night for someone whose evening was meant to be spent at home reading and listening to music. Pratt did that a lot now that he was alone.

He called downtown for more help and got it pretty quickly.

He assigned two new detectives to interview the staff. Several patrolmen were sent out to check nearby alleys and dumpsters for any sign of the murder weapon. Pratt and another patrolman took on the task of questioning the suspect's bandmates.

Pratt knew nothing about what passed for "kids' music" these days, but these three musicians looked the part. One had long hair, two short, but they all looked scruffy, with tattoos, nose rings and torn clothing. They called themselves

Rotten Attitude. All claimed to know "nothing at all."

But beneath their sneers, the detective could tell they were worried and scared. One of their own was downtown, being charged with murder. It was likely that one of them knew something useful. Pratt aimed to find out.

To unnerve them even more, he questioned them one at a time at the far end of the club, where he could be easily seen but not heard. Although he usually sat quietly when questioning a suspect, Pratt made sure this time to gesture a lot and raise his voice. Afterward, he then sent each of them to separate tables to wait, further tightening the screws. They shouldn't have been left together in the first place.

"I can't believe this happened," said the heavyset, long-haired one as he sat down. His earlier bravado was gone, probably because he lacked an audience.

"Name?"

"Mike Master."

"So how long you been in the band, Mikey?" Pratt asked.

Behind the kid, the patrolman taking notes smirked.

"Six months. They asked me to join because they needed a better singer."

"And are you a better singer?"

"Our fans seem to think so."

"So your little band has a lot of fans?"

Pratt was baiting the kid. A bit of anger might cause him to drop his guard.

"If we play our cards right, we'll get a big recording contract. Everyone says so."

Pratt led him through the standard line of questioning. Did he know anything? What had Jamie Clark said? Where was he when the murder occurred? How had Clark behaved that evening?

Master knew nothing—or wasn't about to give up his fellow band member.

The only new thing drummer Jonny Fedrano could add was that Clark had told him before the first set that his knife was missing. Lewis was still alive at that point. Pratt wondered if it was just to set up an alibi.

Bassist Skip Blair was more forthcoming.

"Jamie is innocent! Sure he talks big, but I've known him since we were ten. He'd never hurt anyone, I swear it!"

"Has Jamie ever been involved in a fight?"

"Never that I've seen."

"That sounds like a cop-out."

"It's not, man! Okay? He's my bro."

Pratt wondered what this punk would have said if he'd told him, "No. He's not your bro. My partner is actually Jamie's bro. What do you think of that?" But all he said was, "Look, I'm at least marginally on Jamie's side. Why don't you help me?"

The kid glared at him, making it clear there wouldn't be help.

Could it mean Jamie's band members also thought he was guilty?

* * *

About quarter to three, Pratt was rubbing his tired eyes when someone tapped him on the shoulder. It was one of the crime scene techs.

"Got something to show you downstairs."

"What?"

"You'll see."

Pratt nearly told the guy off, but that seemed like too much effort, so he just followed along.

Downstairs, the office was now almost empty. Only the desk, the chair and a photocopy machine remained. The piles of paper, bar supplies and other junk had all been removed and stacked neatly outside.

"So what do you have?" Pratt asked irritably.

"It was underneath the photocopier. I knew we should have looked there first instead of wasting our time with the other junk."

"Show me, please."

The other tech rolled the copier away and there it was: a rather long switchblade with a carved wooden handle and brass hardware. It was just as Jamie Clark's knife had been described to Pratt by his band members. The blade was still extended.

"There's blood on it," one of the techs said unnecessarily.

CHAPTER FOUR

Pratt didn't drag his sorry butt into the squad room until nearly ten the next morning.

By that time, Jamie Clark had been booked for murder and Harry Gordon was strutting around like a hero. Gordon's partner, Snow, was still sick at home, so Pratt remained on the case.

Ellis was at his desk working the phones for a case they were just finishing up. His desk faced his partner's, and as Pratt sat, Ellis raised his eyebrows in a question.

"Care for a coffee?" the older man asked.

Ellis got off the phone. "Sure. I need to stretch my legs."

The cafeteria was in the basement. They remained silent until they were alone in a far corner of the room.

"Late night?" Ellis asked.

"Got home at four. I'm exhausted."

"So, ah, what did you find out?"

Pratt took a sip of coffee. "Your half brother has been arrested and charged with murder. A switchblade that might be his was found in Lewis's office early this morning, under a photocopier. We believe it's the murder weapon."

Ellis sagged. "Jesus Christ…"

"That's not all. Jamie was not quiet about his dislike of the murder victim. The club manager who found Lewis's body confirmed he'd witnessed an earlier argument between the two. So did two other employees."

"What was it about?"

Pratt grimaced over a large sip of coffee.

"Money, what else? Lewis actually wanted the band to pay to play there."

"That's the way it's done in some of the top clubs. Bands are willing to pay to play, or at least play for nothing, just to be seen."

"Unbelievable! Are they nuts?"

"No. Just desperate. Did you find out anything that might help Jamie?"

"David," Pratt said. Using his partner's first name was not something he often did. "This is where we stop. You can't know anything about this case. You can't come near it. Understand me? If you're really smart, you'll go right upstairs, tell McDonnell about your relationship to Jamie Clark and asked to be moved to another department for the duration."

"I'll think about it."

"Do more than think." Pratt looked at his watch. "Got to go. Gordon and I are meeting with the old man and someone from the DA's office."

As he rose, Ellis grabbed his arm.

"Keep me in the loop, please."

"I'm sorry. I can't do that."

Pratt grabbed his half-finished coffee and headed for the door. Ellis sat there for a minute longer, thinking that it was pretty funny Pratt called McDonnell "the old man" when Pratt was actually five years older than their captain.

* * *

Pratt arrived last. Captain McDonnell and Gordon were already seated at the conference table with another man and woman. The assistant DA was a new face, still green if Pratt was any judge, and he'd brought a secretary or colleague of some sort.

"How nice of you to join us, Mervin," Gordon said with a smirk.

Everyone in homicide knew Pratt didn't like his given name, and most never used it. Gordon made sure he did—whenever he got the chance.

"Pratt," the captain said, "this is Dan Cheevers. He's going to prosecute the case. Gordon has been filling us in on the murder suspect. What have you got by way of background?"

Pratt put on his reading glasses. "Not a whole lot. By the time I arrived, all the patrons had left the club. Only the bar's staff and the band remained. Oh, and the girl-friend of the suspect and two of her friends."

"They were gone when I got there," Gordon added defensively. "Ran like rats deserting a sinking ship. Probably half had drugs on them, if I know the average clubgoer."

Pratt ignored the comment. "We inter-viewed all staff members and the band. I also interviewed Clark's girlfriend, Carolyn Tucci. Around three AM, the crime tech guys discovered what we believe might be the murder weapon. Clark had a similar knife that he said had gone missing earlier yesterday evening."

Gordon interrupted. "It is the murder weapon, dammit! Can't you see Clark's guilty as sin, Pratt?"

Pratt raised an eyebrow.

"Oh, he's confessed? I hadn't heard."

"Enough!" McDonnell barked. He looked at Pratt. "I want this wrapped up fast. We've looked bad in the club district the past few months." Then his ire shifted to Gordon. "But I also want this done right. We can't afford a screwup. Pratt and Gordon, you're on this until further notice. Gordon's the lead. Got that?"

"What about Snow?" Gordon asked. "He's not going to be out sick for long."

"He can team up with Pratt's partner, Ellis."

Cheevers finally spoke up.

"When will forensics report on the knife? This case is weak unless we can tie that knife to the kid."

"Relax," said Gordon. "Pratt, did you find anyone who would swear that Clark was in the washroom the whole time between sets as he claims? The time when Lewis was stabbed to death?"

Pratt knew better than to tell him the girlfriend, Tucci, had told Pratt precisely that. She swore Clark had spent the entire break in the men's room because he felt ill. Pratt couldn't begin to imagine Gordon's response if he said that out loud.

CHAPTER FIVE

Ellis was out when Pratt got back to his desk. He hoped the kid had finally gotten the message that he had to stay far away on this one. It would end badly for everyone if he didn't.

Pratt wanted to study photos of the body. None had arrived yet. As he reached for his phone, its loud ring caused him to jump. His nerves always got jangly when he'd had too little sleep, and that irritated him.

The voice at the other end had a buzz-saw quality that made him wince. "Detective Pratt?"

"Yes."

"Finally! I have been sent from person to person trying to find someone who could tell me about my husband's...death."

"And you are?"

"Margerie Lewis, the wife of...the widow of Joseph Lewis. Are you the one heading the investigation of my husband's death?"

"No, ma'am, but I am working on the case."

"Can you tell me anything? The officer who was sent to my home last night couldn't tell me much."

This call should have been handled by Gordon, but he was over at forensics, bugging them about the knife. He seemed to think pissing people off would get him quicker results.

"There isn't a whole lot to tell you at this point."

"The TV is saying someone has been arrested."

"That's true."

"And did he stab Joe to death?"

Pratt squeezed his eyes shut. Time to take one for the team.

"We have strong reasons to believe that."

The Widow Lewis's next question astounded him. "When can The Boom Room reopen?"

He would have expected an emotional outburst along the lines of "Fry the bastard!" or possibly some weeping. After all, she'd just lost her husband. Frankly, she sounded only mildly irritated.

"May I come over and speak with you?" he asked.

"I want you to answer my question."

"I have no answer at this time. Perhaps by the time I get there, I will know more."

"As you can imagine, I'm very busy today. When would you come?"

"I can be there within the hour."

"Fine. Suit yourself—if it will help speed things up."

"Thank you very much, Mrs. Lewis. See you shortly."

Pratt sat drumming his fingers on his desk after hanging up the phone. Something wasn't right here.

Before heading out to the Lewis house, Pratt got a promise from forensics that the crime scene photos would be on his desk by midafternoon. He hated looking at them on a computer screen.

* * *

Margerie Lewis obviously cared very much about the way she looked. Close to Pratt's age—meaning pushing fifty-five—the blonde (from a bottle) answered her door dressed as if she was going out on the town. She wore a simple black dress with a colorful scarf around her neck. She did not look like a newly minted widow.

"Now, what can you tell me about my husband's murder?" she asked, sitting primly on the sofa.

Pratt got out his notebook and pen.

"We have a suspect in custody, and I believe he has been formally charged or will be shortly."

"Is that the boy from the band?"

"Yes, ma'am. How did you know that? It hasn't been released to the press yet."

"I spoke to the bar manager this morning. He told me."

The detective filed that information away. Who had called whom? he wondered.

"Why are you so interested in talking to me, detective?" she continued. "You've already got your murderer."

"Just doing my job." Pratt crossed one leg over the other so he could write more easily. "Did your husband ever talk to you about the club?"

Margerie rolled her eyes. "All the time. I think he cared more about that dump than he did about me."

"Did he have trouble with people in the past?"

"Do you mean did he get along with people?"

"Well, yes."

"He was a good businessman. That sometimes meant lowering the boom on an employee or supplier. Bartenders and waitresses will rob you blind if you don't watch them constantly. Suppliers will try to rip you off."

"Did he currently have any problem employees?"

She paused to think. "Joe didn't mention anyone recently."

Twenty minutes later, Pratt had poked around enough with his questions to know there was something not being said.

"You asked on the phone when the club could be reopened and—"

"I need to have that dump open, detective. I will be selling it." She tried a smile. "Kids are a fickle lot. They'll find someplace else to go if The Boom Room stays shut too long—and they won't come back. I need a buyer while it's hot."

"Right now it's an active crime scene. We're working as fast as we can."

Mrs. Lewis didn't look happy. "I'm sure you are."

Pratt closed his notebook and rose to his feet. Putting on his coat, he asked, "Tell me, is it hard to sell a nightclub?"

"I hope not. I have zero interest in owning one."

I'll just bet you don't, Pratt thought as he started his car to head back downtown.

It might be well worth the effort to dig around in the Lewis family closet. He'd never met a widow who had appeared less broken up over her husband's murder.

CHAPTER SIX

Back at the office, Pratt got busy writing up his notes from the previous evening. Every detective he'd ever worked with hated paperwork, but he found it soothing—and useful. Many times in the past he'd had breakthroughs while organizing his thoughts for the record.

McDonnell startled Pratt when he dropped a manila envelope on his desk. "These came for you while you were out." He turned on his heel and went back to his office, clearly not happy about something.

The eight-by-ten crime scene photos were crisp and clear. Pratt thumbed through them. He was down to the last half dozen before he found what he was looking for.

Pratt knew the trick was not to simply look. The trick was to see. Last night he hadn't known enough when he'd glanced into that office. He'd looked at things, sure, but he hadn't understood what they might mean. It wasn't until this morning that it had struck him. Something about Lewis's body was odd. Three of the photos told the story.

"What you looking at?" It was Ellis, back from wherever he'd gotten off to.

Pratt turned the photos over. "You know what they are."

His partner sat down, took out his laptop and opened it. "Relax. I didn't see a thing."

"Where have you been?"

Ellis looked at him for a long moment. "Doing some thinking."

"And?"

He sighed. "I've told the captain I need time off to be with my family. He's going to see what he can do."

"You've made the right decision, son. I was going to tell McDonnell if you didn't."

"He told me you're staying on the case even after Snow comes back."

"That surprised me. He knows how much Gordon and I dislike each other."

"Maybe he wants your brains with Flash's brawn."

Pratt smiled, but it was tight. "He sort of said that."

"Can I ask you one thing about the case?"

"Maybe..."

"Mom and Dad spoke to Jamie this morning for just a moment in court. He swears he didn't do it. Sure, he was sore at Lewis, but he was just sounding off."

"Every murderer claims they're innocent. You know that."

"Mom says she can see in his eyes Jamie's telling the truth."

"That should really convince a jury."

"My mother is a realist. She's also very strong. She wouldn't shy away from the truth like most people. May I ask you my question?"

"Sure."

"Gut-level response: do you think Jamie murdered Lewis?"

Ellis already had his mentor pegged. He knew when something was bothering Pratt. They sat for a good half minute before the older man spoke.

"We shouldn't talk here."

* * *

There was a coffeehouse and juice bar they both liked a few blocks from headquarters. For Pratt, it was the coffee and chocolate-chip cookies. For Ellis, the smoothies. Not many cops used the place.

They'd barely sat down when Ellis asked, "So what do you have?"

Pratt looked at his young partner carefully, trying to read him. He had a lot of regard for the young man. The kid showed great instincts and, more important, was willing to put up with Pratt's moodiness.

They were both on dangerous ground. At this stage, Pratt didn't give a damn if he got shown the door. He had a good pension and not much he wanted to spend it on. He'd miss the work, but the end was in sight anyway.

Ellis, on the other hand, was just starting out. He had a career ahead of him. Possibly a brilliant career. There was a young wife too, and, no doubt, children on the horizon.

He took a deep breath.

"All right, David, there is something bothering me about the case."

Pratt had stuffed the three photos of interest into the envelope as they'd left. He took his time laying them out on the small table, studying them once again. Then he turned them one by one to face Ellis.

"What do you notice?"

Knowing this teacher/student game very well, Ellis took his time.

"There isn't much blood?"

Shaking his head, Pratt said, "Dig deeper. Come on, it's right there."

A couple of minutes passed.

"Lewis's hand is on the phone?"

"Okay. What does that tell you?"

Frowning, Ellis stared at the photos. The answer that immediately sprang to mind was that Lewis was calling for help. But he knew that wasn't what his partner had seen.

He slumped.

"I give up."

"Imagine the scene with me. You've had this kid in your face already that day. He was very aggressive too, and had to be pulled away by his band members. Now, the only place the kid could stand in that pigsty of an office is in the doorway. With all that going on, don't you find it odd Lewis would turn his back to make a phone call—for any reason?"

"So you're saying—"

"That Lewis had no reason to fear the person in the doorway, the person who would stick a knife in his back a moment later. That doesn't sound like a description of your brother, does it?"

CHAPTER SEVEN

Ellis headed out on another "errand," but Pratt felt sure his young partner was going to pass news to his mother. He hoped the kid had enough sense not to compromise the case.

His desk was a sea of reports related to the case. It appeared Gordon had decided Pratt should be the one to handle the paperwork. Typical.

Searching his own notes, he found a phone number and dialed. It was time to speak to The Boom Room's manager again.

Carl Thomson answered his cell on the first ring. From the background noise, he was obviously in a bar.

"Mr. Thomson, Detective Pratt here."

"What the hell do you want?"

"I'd like to speak with you again. Can you come down to police headquarters?"

Laughter in the background. "When?"

"As soon as possible, actually."

"Why do you need to speak to me?"

"I can fill you in on that when you get here."

"Is this necessary? I'm sort of busy right now."

I'll bet you are, Pratt thought. "Would you like me to send a cruiser to pick you up?"

"No, no. I can make it there on my own. Is a half hour okay?"

"That should be fine. We're on the fourth floor. Tell them at the desk. Someone will bring you up."

Pratt smirked as he hung up. He'd been pretty sure the offer of a pickup would get Thomson to agree to come quickly.

* * *

The front-desk officer who escorted Thomson up had a smile on her face.

Pulling Pratt aside, she said, "The cheeky bastard tried to pick me up while we were in the elevator!"

"He does seem to think a lot of himself."

"Good luck with him," she said over her shoulder, still chuckling.

"Thank you for coming in so promptly," Pratt said as he took his seat across the table in an interview room and turned on the tape recorder.

"You've caught the murderer, right?"

"Someone is under arrest, yes."

"Then why do you need to speak to me?"

"We're just crossing the t's and dotting the i's."

"Can we make this quick then? I had to leave an important meeting."

Thomson didn't seem worried as he slouched back in his chair—anything but.

This was a fishing trip. With luck, Pratt might net some interesting info.

"I spoke to Margerie Lewis this morning—"

"Before or after I spoke to her?"

Smooth move. Carl Thomson was obviously not stupid.

"How well do you know her?"

"Not well at all. She didn't come down to the club more than once or twice. Not her kind of place, if you know what I mean."

Pratt smiled. "And yet you called her this morning."

"Did she say that? She called me."

"Really? Why?"

"She wanted to find out when the club will open. She thought I'd know."

"Anything else?"

Thomson looked more wary. "I suppose I should have told you last night—"

"Told me what?"

"That I'd offered to buy The Boom Room a month or so ago. Margerie Lewis wanted to know if I'm still interested."

"I see."

Pratt let Thomson hang for a bit as he considered whether this was about damage control. Thomson might be worried Margerie had told him about the offer.

The manager added, "But old man Lewis wouldn't sell. I've been looking for another club to invest in ever since."

"You were disappointed he wouldn't sell?"

"Of course I was. He didn't know his ass from his elbow when it came to what the kids want to hear. I do. I'm the one who made the place a success."

"And last night you found your boss's body."

"You're full of it if you think I had anything to do with it. Ask the head cook.

I was downstairs for all of fifteen, maybe twenty seconds. I found him, freaked and ran back upstairs. We went back down together. Ask him!"

"That short a time? Didn't you check to see if he was dead?"

"He wasn't moving. I told you all this last night."

"I think you left out a few important details."

"Look, I'm not going to say anything more without a lawyer. I didn't do it! It was that kid in the band. He had a big hate-on for Lewis, and he had a wicked-looking knife he said he would use."

"Those were Jamie Clark's exact words?"

"Maybe not exactly, but pretty close. He meant it that way."

The door of the interview room burst open and Gordon stood there.

He didn't look happy either. A lot of people seemed to be in a bad mood that day.

CHAPTER EIGHT

"Just what the hell do you think you're doing, Pratt?" Gordon asked as soon as Carl Thomson had been hustled out the door.

They were still in the interview room. Pratt knew this could get ugly.

"It's called doing my job. I'm not convinced you've got the right person."

"You're not convinced? Just who the hell do you think you are?"

That got Pratt right in Gordon's face. "Listen here, Flash," he said, using Gordon's hated nickname. "Even if it turns out you're right, don't you think it makes sense to check out all possible leads? Do you really want to hitch your wagon to only one horse? Are you that stupid?"

The interview-room door opened again. McDonnell glared at them.

Fifteen minutes later, the captain had made it very clear how things stood. If Pratt wanted to dig around, fine, but he had to let Gordon know what he was doing. And McDonnell wanted to know what both of them were up to. Period.

McDonnell turned to Gordon.

"Has the kid confessed?"

Gordon sagged a bit.

"No. His lawyer won't let him say much."

"I was looking at Pratt's breakdown of what happened during those interviews last night. The girlfriend swears the kid was in the bathroom at the time Lewis was stabbed. I'd suggest you talk to her."

"I was thinking the same thing, boss," Gordon answered.

Pratt knew he probably wasn't. He probably hadn't even looked at Pratt's notes.

"Let me know what you come up with." McDonnell looked at each of them. "You two play nice or you may find I'll buddy you up for keeps. Got it?"

* * *

Ellis was sitting impatiently on a bench outside courtroom nineteen. His request for time off had come through. He only had one last item to finish up—testifying at the Dobbin trial (a small-time hood who'd beaten a musician to death). Since his part in the case had been small, he expected to be on the stand for not more than an hour, maybe two.

From his pocket came the theme from *Dragnet*. He pulled out his phone and said simply, "Ellis."

The voice at the other end was female. "Um, I got your number from your mother."

"Who is this?"

"My name is Carolyn Tucci, and I'm your brother Jamie's girlfriend. I live with him."

Ellis was not happy. He needed to be focused for court.

"And you're calling me for what reason?"

"I didn't know who else to turn to. I have some information. It might help Jamie."

"My partner is working on the case. He can help you. His name is—"

"Detective Pratt. Yes, I've met him. I don't want to talk to some old fa—"

"You need to talk to him," Ellis broke in. "I can't have anything to do with this case. I'm a cop. Jamie is my half brother. There's a conflict."

"I'm reaching out to you because you are his brother. Please! Will you listen to what I know?"

A guard stuck his head out the door, signaling Ellis that they were ready for him.

"I'm about to go into court. I'll call you when I'm done. Okay?"

She sighed. "I guess so."

CHAPTER NINE

Nearly three hours later, Ellis had to wait while her phone rang four times before she answered.

"Hello?"

"Detective Ellis. Now what do you want to tell me?"

"Oh…damn. I'm in the middle of my shift."

There was the loud sound of steam in the background. He guessed she worked in a coffee shop.

"Tell me why you called."

"I can't talk now, but I'm off in an hour. Can I meet you then?"

"Where are you?"

Her workplace wasn't too far away and there was an outdoor store nearby. He could waste an hour checking out camping gear.

Ellis stood outside the coffee shop, watching his brother's girlfriend as she waited on her last two customers. She had a nice smile. Going inside, he waited until she came over.

"I'm David Ellis."

"I don't want to talk here. I hope you don't mind. I haven't told anyone about Jamie."

"Not a problem."

"There's a burger place that doesn't stink down the street. I'm starved. Would that be okay?"

Ellis was hungry too, but his wife would be home tonight—and cooking dinner. "Not a problem."

Beneath the goth "look at me" makeup, Carolyn Tucci seemed like a nice enough kid, probably fresh from the suburbs. She was wearing tight black jeans and a cropped black T-shirt that only emphasized her skinny body. Her mother probably worried about how she was eating. By the way she tucked into her cheeseburger, though, Carolyn probably only needed to grow into her adult body.

While she ate, he could almost see the wheels turning in her head. From the little Pratt had said, he knew that she was smart and quick, but was she honest? He'd never been impressed with Jamie's friends before. Was she another of those?

"It's so weird to be talking to you…" she began as she wiped away a blob of ketchup from the corner of her mouth.

"Why?"

"You're Jamie's brother, but you're so different from him."

"Why? Because I'm a cop?"

"Partly, I suppose. Jamie hates cops."

"That's because he hates me."

She leaned across the table. "You're just like every other cop. You all think Jamie's guilty."

"If I thought that, I wouldn't have bothered to meet you, would I?"

Carolyn picked up a fry and popped it in her mouth. As she chewed, her gaze was faraway.

"Jamie told me once he doesn't think anyone in his family really knows who he is. Jamie's not like other guys. At his core, he's sensitive and kind—and very talented. You've never heard songs like his. I like just reading his lyrics. They're real poetry."

Ellis thought of his brother's music as nothing more than noise. He kept his mouth shut.

She dabbed another fry in the puddle of ketchup on her plate.

"Most guys I know are total dicks. They only look at girls as an easy lay. Jamie's not like that. I want to help him if I can."

Ellis tried to keep the surprise he felt at her words out of his voice.

"Do you have something that will help him?"

"Jamie was in the can the entire time between the first and second sets last night. I know. I was out in the hall waiting for him. He couldn't have knifed Lewis."

"You told my partner that last night. I'm sorry, but it's not something that will stand up in court unless you have another witness."

"But it's the truth!"

Ellis shrugged, feeling this was all a waste of time. "You're his girlfriend. They would expect you to say that. Anything else?"

Carolyn leaned forward again.

"You might want to check out Mike Master."

"Why?"

"Because he's mega strange."

"That's not a lot to go on."

"Since he joined the band, he's said a lot of things about where he came from, things he did. I looked it up on the Internet this morning. It was complete BS. There's no record of him anywhere I could find. Not in the town he claims to come from, not in the county, not anywhere."

"So you're an expert at using the Internet to find people?"

"I know my way around. Want me to prove it? Maybe I'll look you up."

"I didn't mean that as an insult. That's a skill set most people don't have."

"Well, I do!" She picked up a fry and used it as emphasis. "Either Mike's lying about his name or lying about where he's from. That's suspicious. And like I told you, he's a mega-strange dude. You need to check him out."

CHAPTER TEN

Pratt thought there was nothing of the budding rock star as Jamie Clark was led into the interview room at the city jail. Dressed in an orange jumpsuit, he just looked like what he was. A scared twenty-two-year-old.

"Who are you?"

"Detective Pratt. I'm one of the people investigating the murder of Joseph Lewis."

"Shouldn't I have my lawyer here?"

"You can, of course. But then my questions will have to wait until at least tomorrow. You're in a deep hole, and right about now they're starting to fill it in.

Tell you what. If I ask a question you don't want to answer, just tell me to piss off, okay?"

Under the desk, Pratt crossed his fingers. Did he have the kid pegged right?

Clark slouched back in his chair. His shoulders rose and fell once.

Pratt nodded, then pulled out his notebook and pen.

"I know what you said in your statement, so we don't need to cover that. But I have a few questions about what happened earlier in the day. Take this missing knife of yours. Can you tell me positively the last time you had it?"

Jamie pursed his lips. "I used it to cut some pieces of gaffer's tape when we were setting up our gear."

"What time was that?"

"Sometime after five. That's when load-in is."

"What happened to the knife after you used it?"

"I put it back in my pocket."

"Are you sure?"

"I'm very careful with that knife."

Pratt didn't bother to mention that having it was completely illegal.

"You don't remember having it any time after that?"

"No."

"When did you discover it was missing?"

"When we were getting changed in the dressing room. Look, most of this is in my statement."

"I know. I'm just trying to get more details about that knife." Pratt looked down at his notebook, even though he was making this up as he went along. "What did you say when you discovered it was missing?"

"I asked the rest of the band, didn't I? Look, I wasn't in the best of moods. Lewis was being a prick about money. And then he wouldn't let us do a soundcheck."

"Who was in the club at the time you last saw the knife?"

"The band, Carolyn and a friend of hers. There were two guys stocking the bar. Carl the manager. Lewis. There might have been some people in the kitchen."

"When you used the knife to cut the"— Pratt glanced down at his notebook— "gaffer's tape, who might have seen it?"

"Anyone in the band, I suppose. Carl was hanging around, talking to us. He's been angling to manage the band. Thinks he's an operator." Jamie leaned forward suddenly. "Why are you asking me all these questions about the knife? What gives?"

"I'm just trying to account for its where-abouts during the time you were in the club."

"Does this mean I'm not completely screwed? I got the feeling you cops have it in for me. I know all about cops. I have a half brother who's one."

"I wouldn't talk about that if I were you."

"In here? Are you kidding? Do you think I'm that stupid?"

"No. I'm talking about saying it anywhere. If I were you, I wouldn't tell anyone. It won't help you."

"I know he'll think I'm guilty."

Pratt shook his head. "No, he doesn't think that at all."

"Bullshit."

"Believe it or not, I'm telling you the truth." Pratt leaned forward. "But getting back to your earlier question, son, you will get buried if you murdered Joseph Lewis. I'm just trying to make sure we have the truth."

CHAPTER ELEVEN

On opposite sides of the city in the early hours of the morning, Detectives Pratt and Ellis pushed their chairs away from their computers and rubbed tired eyes.

Pratt was in the squad room, having thoroughly checked out Margerie Lewis, her husband and the club's manager, Carl Thomson. Searching police records had uncovered a few interesting tidbits. Thomson had once been arrested for domestic violence, but charges were later dropped. He'd also once been linked to a biker gang. Joseph Lewis had been investigated for fraud a number of years back. But the case had never made it to court. Margerie Lewis at first appeared to be an upstanding member of the community. But then he'd found her named in a divorce suit six years ago. She had been married to Lewis at the time.

It wasn't a lot to go on, but it did show that two of the three had possibly operated on the windy side of the law at one point or another. The only way to move forward now was to do some good old legwork.

But first, Pratt definitely needed a few hours of shut-eye.

Ellis, on the other hand, was completely wired. He sat alone in his spare bedroom as his wife slept. He'd found nothing about Mike Master anywhere in the country. On the Internet, the guy simply didn't exist. It felt odd to be so happy about something not found.

Rolling the desk chair back toward his laptop, he muttered, "All right. I know you're out there somewhere. Let's find out who you really are…"

* * *

Pratt rolled into work the next morning at nine twenty, his eyes still smarting from two days of little sleep and long hours staring at a computer screen.

He was soon on his way again. Armed with photos of Margerie Lewis and Carl Thomson, he drove out to the suburban neighborhood where the Lewises lived.

Pratt first tried his luck at the house directly across the street. An old woman answered the doorbell. Perfect. Maybe she was the "nosy neighbor" type.

His badge in his hand, he said, "I'm Detective Pratt. We're searching for a man, and I'm hoping you can help."

"What man? Why?"

Pratt pulled out his photos of Thomson. "This man. Have you seen him in the area?"

She looked at them long and hard, then shook her head.

"No. I don't believe I've ever seen him before."

"It would probably be during the day."

Now she was more certain.

"No. Sorry I can't help. Is he dangerous?"

"No. We just want to ask him some questions. Sorry to have bothered you."

At the surrounding houses, Pratt had two no-answers to his ring and two more negative answers from people who came to their doors. He might have continued down the street, but if the immediate neighbors hadn't seen anything, he doubted he'd get any hits farther away.

Thomson's face was also unknown to the old man living in the house directly backing onto the Lewises'. On either side of him, it was the same. At that point, Pratt gave up, somewhat depressed. It had been a bit of a long shot, but he'd had hopes.

At the far end of the street was the back end of a fairly large park. Pratt figured he'd try his luck there. Not wanting to alarm the young mothers he found near the playground, he told them it was an insurance-fraud case.

After twenty minutes, he'd struck out again. Spotting a park bench, he sat to reconsider his theory. Maybe he was barking up the wrong tree.

The sun was warm, so he unbuttoned his overcoat. It was finally feeling like spring.

A few minutes later, a young mother sat down at the other end of the bench. She needed to tend to her fussy baby. Once a bottle was stuck in its mouth, the crying stopped. The mother sighed, shut her eyes and tilted her head back, bathing her face in the warm sun.

A moment later, she asked without opening her eyes, "You a cop?"

Pratt sat up straight. "What makes you think that?"

"You look like one. I know the breed. My dad's a cop too. Maybe you know him. His name's Burt McDonnell. He's a detective."

"You're Shelley McDonnell? Excuse me, but I didn't recognize you. Actually, the last time I saw you, you were only twelve."

She finally turned, and sure enough, he could detect a bit of her dad in her eyes and mouth. "And you are?"

"Pratt. Merv Pratt," he answered, holding out his hand.

As they shook, she grinned.

"My dad's mentioned you. Says you're a real good detective, but a pain in the ass. I hope you don't mind my saying that. Dad's pretty blunt, as you certainly must know."

Like father, like daughter, he thought.

Shelley tilted her head to the sun again. "What brings you here? Are you hot on a case right now?"

"Something like that. I'm trying to find out if someone has been seen around this neighborhood."

"Any luck?"

"So far, no."

"Who is it?"

"This guy," Pratt said, holding out one of the Thomson photos.

She looked at it for only a second.

"I've seen him a few times. He drives a yellow 'Vette. Nice car, the kind you notice. He leaves it on the far side of the park, then cuts across, walks down the street and around the corner. An hour or so later, he's back."

"Is he always alone?"

"As far as I've seen. Bet he's canoodling with some lonely housewife in the neighborhood. He looks the type," she added, handing back the photo. "So, is marital infidelity now on official police radar?"

"Not really. I'm trying to find out if he knows someone a bit better than he admits."

"On the way back to his car, he looks like a canary-swallowing cat, so I'd say yes."

Pratt got to his feet. "Thanks for your help, Shelley."

"No problem. Small world, isn't it?"

"You can say that again." He started to walk away, then turned. "By the way, when was the last time you saw our friend?"

She pursed her lips, considering. "About a week ago. Yes. A week ago Friday. He was a bit longer that day. Looked as if he had a pretty good romp."

Shelley flashed Pratt a big smile, then turned to her baby, who'd finished the bottle.

Pratt's step had more life in it as he walked back to his car.

CHAPTER TWELVE

Ellis was also in a park. He'd slept only three hours, but unlike his older partner, he felt wide awake, ready for anything.

At nine AM, he'd gotten hold of Carolyn Tucci to arrange another meeting. She had an earlier shift that day, and they agreed to meet in a park near the coffee shop.

As she walked up, he studied her closely. Underneath all the goth makeup and facial piercings, she reminded him strongly of the mother he and Jamie shared. He wondered if his half brother realized that.

Ellis got right to the point. "Tell me more about Mike Master."

"What have you found out?"

"Pretend I know nothing. I want to hear this in your words."

"Well, he's weird, very weird."

"You said that yesterday. Can you be more specific?"

"He lies about everything. Have you seen his Facebook page?"

Ellis nodded.

She continued, "Since he joined Rotten Attitude—"

"When was that?"

"About eight months ago. Since he joined, I've heard him change stories about things dozens of times. The band just writes it off as him being a born bullshitter, but I'm not so sure. Here's something else: he has no ID. I looked in Mike's wallet once, and there was nothing in it but a bit of cash. No cards, no driver's license, no nothin'. Do you know anyone with zero ID in this day and age?"

"Where does he live?"

"At the band house. Jamie and I have our own place now, but the rest of the guys live at the house. They rehearse in the basement. They think it's cool, but it's really a dump and not worth the rent."

"How does everyone in the band get along?"

"Pretty well, I guess. Of course, they have fights about songs when they're working them out. Nothing serious though. Jamie writes all the band's good songs." She reached in her purse and pulled out a CD. Its cover had only *Rotten Attitude* scribbled across it. "Promise me you'll listen to it. It's really good."

Ellis nodded and slipped it into his coat pocket. "How does Jamie get along with Mike?"

She shrugged. "All right, although there's a lot of push and pull over who's the leader of the band. Mike obviously wants to be."

"And the others?"

"Skip and Jonny have been with Jamie since high school. They're still solid. But with Jamie currently out of the picture, I don't know what will go down."

"What do they believe happened the other night?"

Carolyn sighed heavily.

"I get the feeling they think Jamie did it. They won't say so, of course, but you can see it in their eyes. A couple of weeks ago, we were all sitting around after a long rehearsal. Gigs have been thin on the ground, and Rotten Attitude seems to be spinning its wheels. They were shooting the shit about surefire ways to get noticed. Someone jokingly said, 'Well, I guess one of us could always kill someone.' We all laughed."

"Do you remember who said that?"

She thought for a couple of seconds, then shrugged. "No. Sorry."

"Bet it doesn't seem so funny now."

CHAPTER THIRTEEN

P ratt's luck didn't hold through the afternoon or else the cheating couple had never met around Thomson's apartment. Either way, he now had something to confront them with. Question was, did the husband know?

The next stop downtown was to speak again with The Boom Room's longest-serving employee, a bartender named Ben.

Fittingly, they met at a bar—just not the one Ben hoped he still worked at.

Being midafternoon, the joint was deserted. Ben had a pint, and Pratt, black coffee.

"I need you to help clear up a few questions," Pratt began.

"Hey, no problem. If it will help things along and get The Room open again. Everyone is asking about it."

"You don't think people would be turned off that someone was murdered there?"

"Are you kidding? Now The Room is even more notorious! It'll be jammed from the first night—guaranteed."

Ben looked to be north of thirty with short blond hair, blue eyes and bulging muscles. Pratt guessed why he enjoyed working there. "All those young girls and so little time" was probably the bartender's motto.

Reading from his notes, Pratt said, "When I first questioned you, you told me, quote, 'Joe Lewis really had no idea how a bar operation runs.' Care to elaborate?"

"This is between you and me, right?"

"Absolutely. Nothing will have to come out unless it has a direct bearing on Lewis's murder, and then only in court."

"Well, okay. I just don't want to risk my job."

"So what did you mean about Lewis?"

"He was a businessman, sure. Had some money, bought the club four years ago and figured to rake in the dough. But you have to know things beyond ordering booze and stuff. You gotta know what brings in the crowds. He tried a DJ for a while, but the joint wasn't exactly jumping."

"So what changed? I understand it's now the hottest place in town."

"Carl Thomson. He's got the touch about what's hot and what's not. Carl started booking live acts, got Joe to put in a kick-ass light show. The place changed overnight."

"So what are you gun-shy about telling me?"

"Carl Thomson, he's a shifty bugger."

"Is he dealing drugs out of the place?"

Ben took a pull on his beer.

"Not smart in the club district. Somebody takes a dislike to you, and suddenly the cops appear. Carl's not stupid."

"Then what is going on?"

"It started with the usual diddles anyone pulls working in a bar. Carl always took over the service bar when it got busy. We all knew he was bringing in his own booze. Don't ring it in when you pour it, then pocket the money. It's pretty well undetectable. On a busy weekend, you can easily skim a few hundred each night. I'm certain he was running other scams too. When you work behind a bar for a while, you learn all the tricks."

Pratt felt sure Ben did the same thing.

"You said, 'It started with the usual diddles.' What changed?"

"Some of us felt that over the last few months, Carl was doing his best to run the place into the ground."

"How was he doing that?"

"Mostly by booking bad acts, but he also hired two really crappy bartenders— slow, lazy, bad attitudes. Then two weeks ago, Lewis started being at the club more. The two bartenders were canned, and Lewis hired the replacements. Carl was told to book Rotten Attitude. They've always filled the place."

"Having Lewis there was out of the ordinary?"

"Sure. Old Joe just wanted the money at the end of the night. He was never there to work. Carl was going around with a long face, let me tell you. I got the feeling he was going to be shown the door. But Carl had the touch with the bands, and Lewis couldn't get rid of him without slitting his own throat."

"Did you hear any rumors about the place changing hands?"

"Sure. Carl made no secret he wanted to buy it. Actually, he tried to make it a secret, but when he's had a few drinks, his mouth gets a little loose."

"Anything else?"

"They had a big fight about something last week. I was the only one there at the time, but I went downstairs to the office. The door was shut and they were screaming at each other."

"What day?"

"Friday, I think…Yeah. Friday. My luckiest night of that week." Ben flashed a toothy grin. "Would you believe it? Twins!"

CHAPTER FOURTEEN

Pratt had never been to his partner's condo, though he'd been invited several times.

Jennifer Ellis was not what he expected. In many ways, she was her husband's opposite. He was tall (over six feet); she was short (maybe five three). His hair was dark and short; hers, long, flowing and blond. He was quite handsome; she was sort of plain. When she welcomed Pratt, though, he could tell from her eyes that a very special person lived inside. She taught kindergarten, and he got the feeling that she was very good at it.

"Finally I get to meet the formidable Detective Pratt," she said with a smile. "My husband speaks of practically no one else."

Said husband turned bright red.

When Jennifer went off to fetch beers, Pratt suggested they find someplace private to talk.

"The less anyone knows about this, the better."

Ellis suggested the condo's balcony, even though the night was rather chilly. Early spring often brought winds off the lake.

I know where I'd spend my time if I lived here, Pratt thought when he saw the view.

"So why the big rush to see me?" Ellis asked once the beers had been delivered.

"Forensics came back with an early report on the knife we found."

"And?"

Ellis kept his expression blank, but Pratt could tell he knew what was coming.

"Jamie's fingerprints are on it, as well as blood. No DNA yet, of course, but the blood type is the same as Lewis's."

"Jesus Christ…"

"I shouldn't be telling you this, of course, and I'd suggest you keep it from your family. We're not going to announce it to the press for the moment—unless Gordon shoots off his mouth."

"So that's the end of it."

"Not quite." Pratt opened his briefcase, which contained the police computer Ellis wanted to use. On top were two photos. "They sent over photos, and something on them is bothering me. Take a look at these and tell me what you think."

They were close-ups of the dusted knife. The prosecution would use them in court to identify the accused's fingerprints on the murder weapon.

"There are some odd smudges on the handle just above the blade."

"Good lad. Forensics won't say what they think. Gordon says that's where your brother gripped the blade when he was pulling it out of Lewis's back. That caused the smudges. I can't explain them, and that bothers me. I've never seen anything like it before, frankly."

"What are you going to do with this?"

"Think about it. Try to come up with other ways it could have happened."

Ellis needed access to the police computers, something he didn't have at the moment. So far, he'd been unable to track down any information about Mike Master before he'd joined the band. While that fact was telling, Ellis needed to get some solid information about the singer's past. Pratt's computer was his only hope for that, since he'd had to turn in his while on leave.

It didn't take Ellis long to tell Pratt the little he actually knew. And most of that came from Carolyn Tucci, so it might not be reliable.

Pratt asked, "And you believe Tucci is on to something?"

"I didn't at first. But when I found Masters actually was completely off the radar, I began to think she might be right. Obviously, Mike Master isn't his real name."

"Also, Carolyn might not be privy to everything going on in the band."

"I thought of that too."

"I would talk to Jamie again, but I caught hell from McDonnell for going to see him by myself. If I go again, I have to let Flash tag along. I don't know if I want to do that."

"That only leaves the band members. I'd talk to them—"

"If anyone needs to be questioned, I do it. Period."

Ellis smiled. "Yes, boss." He took a last swig of his beer. Then asked a little too casually, "So how is Jamie?"

"Scared. Gordon is really turning the screws in hopes of getting a confession. I didn't BS him. He's in deep if we don't come up with something. But I did let him know someone's working for the truth."

Ellis sighed. "We all appreciate your efforts."

"The least I can do."

"So how do we proceed?"

"Use my laptop. You can log in as me. You know this computer stuff better than I do. So I'll let you handle searching for Master through official channels." Pratt put down his empty beer bottle. "But I need your help too. I need someone to follow Carl Thomson, someone who won't be seen."

He quickly sketched out what he had learned during the day and what he suspected.

"If we could catch Thomson and Margerie Lewis together, we might make good use of that to get other information. You think Master might be involved with Lewis's murder. I think it might be Thomson and the wife."

"So I follow him, and hopefully they meet up. What then?"

"Call me, and I'll step in. No one needs to know you were involved."

"I like it. But how do we get them to meet?"

"I'm going to light a little fire under them and see what it smokes out. By the way, can you do that cell-phone-records trick again for me? It would be nice to know if they've been calling each other."

* * *

Two hours later, Ellis got up stiffly and stretched out the kinks. Jen had long since disappeared to bed. He found Pratt on the living-room sofa, snoring softly.

Using Pratt's login, Ellis had sent out on the police network two photos from the band's Facebook page. He'd asked for help from anyone who might know the face. As he'd expected, there had been no record of Master's name on the official computers.

Now he'd have to try to be patient, waiting to see if any law enforcement agencies responded to his inquiry.

CHAPTER FIFTEEN

As Pratt was leaving the condo, the final thing Ellis told him was, "You need to check out Rotten Attitude's Facebook page. It will give you a clearer view of how Master views himself. For one thing, he's a cocky bastard. You'd think he was already a rock star."

In Pratt's case, checking out the page was easier said than done.

He was up and at 'em at seven the next morning. At his kitchen table with his usual toast and coffee, he was prepared to do battle with his laptop.

Pratt knew how to turn it on, and he'd been taught the bare minimum of how to use what he needed for his job. But social media? He'd heard enough about that to curl what hair he had left.

Ellis had emailed detailed instructions on what to do. Pratt munched a piece of cold toast as he read them a second time.

"Seems straightforward enough," he muttered.

Fifteen minutes later, he was ready to chuck the laptop right out the window. Looking at the email again, he started over.

This time, it was a piece of cake. He was sure he'd done exactly the same thing before. That's why he hated computers so much.

After pouring a second cup of coffee, he went through the process of "liking" Rotten Attitude's page. Twenty minutes later, he'd seen enough.

McDonnell had called a meeting for nine, so Pratt had to get a move on. But as soon as he had a chance, he needed to talk to his partner. Had Ellis seen that small slip too?

* * *

"Please tell me we have the murder-weapon situation sewn up," the skipper said as soon as everyone had sat down.

At the conference-room table, Gordon was busy studying the table's surface, Pratt was studying everyone and Cheevers was shuffling papers inside his open briefcase.

"Gordon," McDonnell prompted. "What have you got?"

Gordon slid the two murder-weapon photos across the table to Cheevers.

"There you go. Nice clear prints from our suspect on the knife. Easy peasy."

Cheevers looked at them closely. Pratt's opinion of him went up when he asked, "What about these smudges on the handle?"

"Probably happened when he pulled out the knife," Gordon quickly responded. "My theory is that something spooked the kid.

That's why he threw the knife under the photocopier."

McDonnell asked, "What does the kid say?"

"Nothing anymore without his lawyer on hand—not after what Pratt did."

"Well, I don't like this. I want an answer ASAP."

"Why the rush?" Pratt asked. "I have some other angles I'm currently looking at."

"Turns out the murdered man's widow has friends at City Hall. They're asking when the club will be reopening. Is there any reason it can't?"

Gordon cut in. "I'll get on the blower to find out if Forensics is through."

"The singer for the band, Mike Master, also called—twice. They want their gear back—not that we have to hurry on their account."

As the meeting ended, Pratt badly wanted to talk with Ellis. But there was no time for that now. As he'd looked at the two photos again, something had finally occurred to him. It was a pretty wild theory, and to prove it, he needed to get down to the club before the all clear was given.

He hotfooted it to the street, where he hailed a cab, telling the driver to step on it.

A uniform was still on duty at the door. Forensics wasn't on scene at the moment.

"I think they may be done, sir," the patrolman told the detective. "But we're always the last to know about those things."

The club smelled less of beer and body odor than Pratt remembered. It was still filthy though, as cleaners hadn't been allowed in yet.

He felt sure now that the murder had been a spur-of-the-moment opportunity. The matter of Jamie Clark's heated argument with Lewis had started it off. Someone had seen what happened and used it for his own ends. But why and, more important, who?

The main room had been pretty thoroughly searched before the knife showed up under the photocopier, but in thinking back, Pratt had remembered one spot that hadn't gotten much of a going-over. The stage.

Rotten Attitude's gear was still there, in much the same place he remembered from the night of the murder.

It took a few minutes to get the stage lights on. Their flashing and sweeping movement almost made him ill, but he needed to be able to see.

Pratt began to carefully check each piece. The drum set was fairly easy, but the amplifiers were quite heavy. The effort of moving them into the light soon had him removing his jacket and wiping his brow with his shirt sleeve.

Two of the smaller amps had slightly open backs. Laying the first one facedown, Pratt shone his flashlight around the inside. He found some guitar cords and a small metal box with *The Destroyer* printed on its front. Pratt wondered what it could be used for. Other than the speaker, there was nothing else.

The second amp looked much the same, although it had two smaller speakers covered by a piece of wood that only partially covered the back. Pratt couldn't see much and hadn't brought a screwdriver, so he used his hand to feel around. Almost immediately, he touched something metal stuck to the big magnet on the back of the left speaker.

He knew at once what it was.

CHAPTER SIXTEEN

Forensics responded to Pratt's call with impressive speed.

"I'm not surprised this was missed first time through," the tech said. "Whoever stuck the knife here knew it wouldn't come loose, not with this huge magnet holding it." He removed the final screw holding the back on. "Thing that puzzles me is why you were looking for this in the first place."

"You've seen those smudges on our murder weapon?"

"Yeah. I took the photos."

"What did you think?"

"They bothered me. Gordon had too ready an explanation, seemed to me. If you were pulling the knife out quickly, you might cause those smudges, but I wasn't convinced."

The flashing stage lights had been turned off and two portable work lights set up. The two techs wanted to get this new knife photographed properly in situ.

"How did you figure this out?" the tech asked as he worked.

"I like to consider things backward," Pratt answered. "It often helps."

"Like this time. Man! You're a magician, Pratt."

The knife looked similar to the murder weapon. The handle was different, being all metal, but its blade, once revealed, would almost surely be the same length.

Just then McDonnell showed up— followed closely by Gordon.

"What have you got, Pratt?" he shouted, striding down the length of the room.

"A second switchblade."

Gordon looked like he'd been slapped. "A second knife?"

The tech was ready to remove the knife from the grip of the speaker magnet. The three detectives crowded around to watch.

"How did you come up with this?" McDonnell asked.

"Those smudges on the first knife bothered me. They were odd, not expected. I simply tried to come up with other theories to explain them."

"And that led you to a second knife?"

"I felt from the beginning that the knife we found might be a plant. Consider. You've just stabbed someone. Do you throw the murder weapon away in a place where it will certainly be found?"

Gordon said, "Come on, Pratt. No one said this kid was a brain."

"No, but they didn't say he was stupid either. It just didn't make sense. Then there were the smudges on the handle. What if they got there because someone was holding the knife with two fingers and then wiped off those fingerprints, leaving Clark's alone on the rest of the handle?"

"You couldn't stab someone with just two fingers on a knife. It takes some force."

"Precisely. And that led me to consider another knife and a different murderer."

The tech delicately pulled the knife from the magnet's grip. He placed it on a piece of plastic, then used a small screwdriver to press the blade release button.

"Normally I would wait until we got back to the lab to do this. You deserve to see it though, Pratt." He pulled a magnifying glass from his toolbox. "Yep. There's blood on this blade, although it's been wiped or I'm a rookie."

McDonnell and Pratt both leaned forward to look. Gordon declined.

"So, Pratt," the skipper asked, "who's the guilty party?"

"That I can't tell you yet, but I have a few theories."

"Well, get right to work on it. Gordon will be glad to help you, I'm sure."

McDonnell winked at Pratt as he turned and headed for the door.

Gordon was clearly beside himself with fury but knew enough to keep his mouth shut.

"What do we do now, all-knowing one?" he asked Pratt.

Pratt ignored him and spoke to the tech.

"We need to get this knife identified ASAP. And make sure you dust that speaker magnet too. Space was tight back there. It's likely the person who put it there left some good prints. How soon can you get us prints and photos?"

"Give me your email address. I can download the photos to my laptop and email them right to you. Prints will take a bit longer, but I'll make sure you have them by day's end."

Would wonders never cease? Pratt got the feeling the two techs were rubbing it in

Gordon's face. Flash had a bad name with the support crews.

Pratt's problem was that he had a few likely suspects, but nothing solid to go on yet. He needed to speak to Ellis—pronto.

*   *   *

"Is this Detective Pratt?" the voice on the other end of the line asked.

Ellis willed his heartbeat to remain slow as he held his cell phone to his ear. "No, it isn't. This is his partner." He then added to the fib with an outright lie, since he'd put his number on the police bulletin instead of Pratt's. "He must have left his phone behind again. What can I do for you?"

"I'm responding to a bulletin he put out last night. Could you ask him to give me a call?"

"No problem. Can you ID the person in our two photos?"

"Short answer—yes. Long answer—I only tell Pratt. Just get him to call me, son. Okay?"

Ellis quickly scribbled down the details. Then he hit the Speed-dial key for Pratt. Hopefully, Pratt would pick up when his phone rang, for a change.

Ellis had spent the past few hours tailing The Boom Room's manager around town. Right now he was sitting in his car across the street from a trendy bar. Thomson had arrived and immediately made a phone call.

Thomson had just been served a pint of beer. Then Margerie Lewis arrived, dressed in jeans and a silk shirt. Ellis could see them clearly since their table was front and center in a large window. Pratt was correct. Margerie was definitely not your typical grieving widow as she chatted, gestured and smiled.

So far so good. Ellis snapped several photos. He was sort of enjoying playing private eye.

Why hadn't Pratt called back yet? He was bad about remembering to recharge his phone, so it might be out of juice. Or he might be involved in something that couldn't be interrupted. Ellis sighed. He just had to be patient.

While the Widow Lewis had only a glass of white wine, Thomson was chowing down on a burger and fries. Both leaned across the table at intervals, making it clear they didn't want to be overheard. As the conversation went on, Margerie looked less and less happy. Ellis smacked himself upside the head. Too bad he couldn't hear what they were saying to each other.

He was watching them pay their bill (separate checks, interestingly) when his cell phone rang.

It was Pratt, finally.

"So you've gotten some action on that bulletin you put out? That was quick."

"Problem is, the guy will only talk to you, since I put your name on the bulletin. I didn't think it was, um, smart to impersonate you."

"Very wise. Where are you right now?"

"In my car watching Thomson and Lewis preparing to leave Gill Maloney's Bar and Grill."

Pratt chuckled. "Looks as if my poking around lit a fire under them. When the cops start asking questions of friends or employees, it usually does. You got photos, of course?"

"Natch. Want me to follow one of them? They seem to be going in separate directions."

"No need. I just wanted evidence of them having lied to me about how well they know each other. I can reel them in at my leisure now."

"I got a good shot of them holding hands. But she was looking pretty unhappy by the end of the conversation."

"Great! I knew I could count on you."

Ellis cut to the chase. "We need to get together. You have to call this guy back.

I'm dying to find out what he knows about Master. Where are you right now?"

"Standing outside The Boom Room. My phone's battery needed charging. I borrowed a uniform's cell to call you."

"I'm about fifteen minutes away. I'll buzz over and pick you up."

"We're getting close on this one, David. I can feel it."

CHAPTER SEVENTEEN

Ellis set his phone to *Speaker* and passed it to his partner.

"Detective Sergeant Merv Pratt calling. You called me earlier."

"Ah, yes, Pratt. Your bulletin was passed on to me. I think I know your boy. What's he done this time?"

"First of all, please tell me about yourself. I like to know who I'm talking with."

"Sheriff Martin Warsh. The person in your photographs appears to be Desmond Nolen, although he didn't have long hair and that stupid goatee and mustache when I knew him. Used to be clean-cut."

"And how do you know him?"

"We suspect him of killing a young woman. We could never pin anything on him though. He's a slippery one."

"Whoa, whoa. You're starting at the end. I need to know the beginning and the middle."

"I have the whole thing written up, along with the wanted bulletin. I can fax you everything."

"I'd really appreciate that, Sheriff."

"So why are you boys interested in Nolen?"

"It could be murder. Fax me those notes. I'll go through them and call you back. Okay?"

"Suits me fine. I'll be waiting."

"How fast can you get me to head-quarters?" Pratt asked after the call ended. "I want to be there when that fax arrives. I don't want Gordon getting hold of it first."

"From here, eight minutes if you think I should break a few laws."

"Break a few laws."

As they muscled their way through the downtown traffic, Pratt and Ellis discussed what the order of things should be.

"You should get Gordon to follow up on the Thomson-Lewis angle," Ellis said. "That way you and I can focus on Master."

Pratt was silent for a couple of minutes. "I'm not saying you shouldn't be involved, David, but we need to tread carefully here. You can't be seen to be involved. It's tricky."

"How do we explain the photos I took then? You can't say you took them. You were down at The Boom Room when Thomson met Lewis."

"Hmm…Let me think about that."

"So what are you going to do about Mike Master?"

"I'm thinking that perhaps we should bring the entire band in, turn up the heat and see what pops."

"How about I handle the Tucci girl? I've already spoken to her. She told me she was going to poke around a little more. Maybe she's got new information."

Pratt considered, then nodded.

"That could work. Get in touch with her. If she's got anything else, share it with me at once, okay?"

At police headquarters, Pratt got out of the car, then stuck his head back inside.

"And don't share what's going on with anyone. That includes your family."

Before driving off, Ellis dialed Carolyn Tucci.

She sounded excited. "I was just going to call you."

"About what?"

"All kinds of new information. I went over to see the band today."

Slightly alarmed, Ellis asked, "Did you talk to Master?"

"Mike? Nah. I wanted to ask Jonny and Skip some things. But I did snoop a bit in Mike's room. Can we meet someplace?"

"Sure." It was nearly two. "I'm outside police headquarters. Could we meet at the same park as before?"

"Not a problem. I have to be at work at six anyway. Look for me in half an hour. Got to dash. Someone's at the door."

CHAPTER EIGHTEEN

Gordon wasn't in the squad room when Pratt got up there. He stopped in the doorway of McDonnell's office and waited for him to get off the phone.

"I was just talking with Cheevers. He says to tell you 'well done' on finding that second knife. That goes for me too. Good work."

"Thanks. Where's Gordon?"

"He's gone out to bring in the club manager and the grieving widow. He's latched on to them as the most likely suspects. He asked to take Snow with him, and since that lug was just sitting on his fat rear, I said okay. Where are you on this?"

"I have another angle I'm working. Seems Mike Master, the band's singer, has a dodgy past. I should have a fax waiting with some more information on him."

"Well, carry on, but keep me in the loop."

"Will do, skipper."

As he went to retrieve it, Pratt decided he was happy that Gordon had gone after Thomson and Lewis. He couldn't make too much of a mess of that. His strong-arm approach would probably work well on them. And Snow would keep him from going too far.

He found a seven-page fax in the tray beneath the machine. Rather than sit at his desk and run the risk of being disturbed, he took it into an interview room and shut the door. Based on what he saw as he glanced at the first page, he realized he needed to concentrate.

A half hour later, Pratt sat back and rubbed his eyes. Gobsmacked was how he felt.

Things could be much more serious than he'd imagined.

His first call was downstairs.

"I've got three people you need to round up for me. They all live at the same address. Don't tell them anything other than they're wanted for further questioning. Make it all nice and friendly. Their names are Jonny Fedrano, Skip Blair and Mike Master. Tell your men to go easy, but keep on their toes with Master. If you don't find them at their house, let me know immediately. Here's the address…"

Pratt again looked at the faxed report, sighed and made his second call.

"Sheriff Warsh? Pratt here. I've read your report…Yes, I have a number of questions."

* * *

Ellis waited impatiently at the same park bench for Carolyn Tucci to show up.

He looked at his watch again. Nearly five. Where was she? He tried her phone.

No answer. Checking with information, he found no landline listing for either Carolyn or Jamie. Like many young people these days, they probably relied on cell phones.

By five fifteen, he was getting worried. Ellis didn't know how reliable Carolyn was, but so far she'd shown no signs of being a flake—especially where Jamie was concerned.

At five thirty, he decided to call Pratt. He couldn't believe she'd be this late, not without calling.

Something must have happened— possibly something bad.

CHAPTER NINETEEN

"What do you mean, she hasn't shown up?" Pratt asked.

He'd been away from his desk, filling in McDonnell, and there had been a message waiting when he got back. It was Ellis. He'd called him back as fast as he could punch the numbers in.

"She should have been here by four thirty. It's now an hour later. This isn't like her."

"Do you know where the hell she lives?"

"Only that she lives with my brother someplace other than the house the band rents."

Pratt was shuffling through the large box that held all the records of the case so far. He hadn't had time to organize it, so the thing was a disaster, with reports and photos just stuffed in.

"I'll look for the charge sheet on my computer. Maybe it has the address." Pratt impressed even himself as he found the info in record time. "Crap! It has the band house's address. Now why would the kid have done that?"

"I got the feeling they'd just moved in together recently," Ellis told him. "The coffee shop where she works should have it. I'll try there."

"No, you won't. I'll make that call."

"You're not going to leave me on the sidelines, are you?"

Pratt considered for a moment.

"No. I'll get the address, then snag a squad car and driver. We'll come down to pick you up. Sit tight. Call me pronto if she turns up or you hear from her."

* * *

"So in the opinion of this sheriff, as well as a psychologist who examined Master, what we have on our hands is a borderline psychotic," Pratt told Ellis.

They were in the backseat of a squad car as it sped crosstown as fast as the evening rush would allow.

"So Master killed someone?"

"He's only suspected of it. A young girl, a classmate, back when he was sixteen. It was a brutal killing. She was stabbed multiple times. Our lad is very clever though. A regular Einstein, according to Warsh, and top of his class in school. But given to very bizarre behavior over many years. Warsh only found out about it later, but a school psychologist had examined Nolen a year before and strongly recommended treatment. Our boy is superb at being able to blend in and appear perfectly normal when it suits his needs. Had his parents completely under his thumb and they didn't even know it. By the time Warsh pried the results of the psychological tests out of the school board, the kid had disappeared."

Ellis whistled. "And he used a knife too. Did Warsh have any idea what kind?"

"Most likely a survival knife with a serrated blade. Nolen's parents claim they have no idea where their son is. Warsh believes them."

"Where was he between then and now?"

Pratt shrugged. "No idea, but I'll bet it's an interesting story."

The car's radio squawked.

"They've got two of the three you want, Pratt," the cop in the front seat said.

"Let me guess—Fedrano and Blair."

"Right, sir."

"Find out if they have any idea where Master is."

The tinny voice from the other end said, "The two we've got say the third came in screaming that someone had been in his room. When they said it wasn't them, Master left, slamming the front door so hard, it came off one hinge."

Pratt looked at Ellis.

"How long before we get to that address I gave you?" he asked the uniform driving them.

"Maybe five minutes."

"Call for backup. Tell them not to use sirens and to wait for instructions, okay?"

CHAPTER TWENTY

"We're a block away," the driver told the two detectives in the backseat. "What do you want me to do?"

"Pull over here," Pratt told him. "Where's the backup?"

"Two minutes away."

Ellis, bent over his phone's small screen, told Pratt, "There's an alley behind the apartment building."

"Tell them to go there and keep an eye on the back door," Pratt said. "Ellis and I will go in first. If our boy is here, I don't want to alarm him. He might hurt the girl."

Ellis looked at Pratt. "It might be too late for that."

The driver told them, "We've got two more cars responding, sir."

"One at either end of the street, but not within the block. No one goes in or out—especially the press. I'm sure they've heard all of this. Give me your handheld radio, please. Once we're inside, you come up slowly and secure the front door. Got it?"

The two detectives got out of the car and cautiously approached the five-story brick low-rise from the same side of the street—that way, there was less chance of being spotted if someone was watching.

"You carrying?" Pratt asked his partner as they walked.

"I took my gun from the lockbox in my car's trunk while I was waiting for you to pick me up."

"Good boy. Hopefully, there won't be any need for it today. But be ready."

Both men longed to look up. Carolyn's apartment number was 4A. It could very likely be at the front of the building.

"Just be casual," Pratt said as they entered. "Let me do the talking."

Luck was with them, and the super was in.

"Police, ma'am," Pratt said into the phone. "We need to get in."

"Just a moment. I'll be right there."

Pratt flashed his badge and ID when she came to the door. She stepped aside.

"We just want to talk to one of your tenants. Won't be a minute."

Behind his back, Ellis crossed his fingers.

"Do you want me to come up with you?" she asked.

"Won't be necessary, but thanks for offering."

The detectives got on the elevator and pressed 4.

The elevator was old and slow. The building had clearly seen better days, judging by the graffiti. Still, it was clean and didn't smell of urine. Eventually, the doors opened on the fourth floor.

"Moment of truth," Ellis said in a low voice.

"I'll take the lead," Pratt said. "You back me up."

Apartment 4A was down the short hallway on their left, next to a window that gave the hallway light. They moved forward quickly.

At the door, Pratt knocked. "Miss Tucci? Are you in there?" he asked loudly when he got no response. "Please open up."

Nothing.

He turned to Ellis. "Break it down, but pull back or drop. I'll go through after."

Ellis nodded. The door and frame were made of wood. Being young and strong, he splintered the door next to where the lock was with one good body blow. Since he was off-balance, he went through but quickly rolled to the side. Pratt came through right behind him, gun drawn and ready.

The living room was small and sparsely furnished, but the attention of the two men was immediately drawn to the body in the middle of the floor. A stream of blood ran across the wood and disappeared under a chair.

The dead person, lying flat on his back with a wicked knife in his chest, was Mike Master. Curled in the chair, looking dazed, was Carolyn Tucci. She had cuts on both hands and one on her right shoulder.

Ellis went to her while Pratt used the handheld to summon help.

"We need an ambulance. Make it snappy!"

Carolyn began speaking, her voice wobbly. "He came here. He was very angry with me. He had a knife. We struggled. I knew he would kill me."

Pratt told Ellis to find some towels to help with the girl's bleeding. "And bring her a glass of water."

Ellis soon returned with both.

Pratt asked her, "How did this happen?"

"I...I'm not really sure. We were struggling. He knocked me down. I kicked at him. After that, I don't remember anything."

Sirens could be heard in the distance.

"Help is on the way, Carolyn," Ellis told her. "The wounds aren't too deep. You should be okay."

She turned to look at him. "You're sure? I'm so tired." She squeezed her eyes shut. "I was so stupid to think I could trap him. He was like a wild animal."

"Everything will be okay now."

Tears started falling from the girl's eyes. "Are you sure?"

He nodded. "The nightmare is over."

CHAPTER TWENTY-ONE

Pratt and Ellis led Carolyn Tucci, barefoot, around the perimeter of the room to the paramedics waiting at the door.

Pratt told one of the uniforms in the hall to accompany the girl to the hospital. "And make sure you keep a close eye on her until you hear from me."

"What was that all about?" Ellis asked. "The danger is over."

"You don't get what's going on yet, do you?"

"What am I not getting here?"

"A lot. Come on. We're going back downtown. Let the boys do their work in peace."

The older man pulled him over to the side of the hall to let the forensics team through. As the lead passed, Pratt pulled him aside, telling him to get prints off the body right away.

"And that glass on the side table. I want prints off that too. Some are Ellis's, but the others are the girl's. I need everything on my desk, like, right now. Can you do that for me?"

"Sure. Shouldn't be a problem, Pratt."

Pratt borrowed Ellis's phone and was on it most of the drive back to headquarters. The younger detective remained mystified by his mentor's behavior.

On the sidewalk, Ellis stood in front of his partner, blocking the way. "What the hell is going on? Master is dead. We got our man."

Pratt put his arm around Ellis. "Come upstairs with me. All shall be revealed."

Ellis refused to move. "Just tell me one thing first."

"Sure. Fire away."

"Is Carolyn Tucci a goddamned suspect?"

"Yes."

"How the hell is that possible? And how did I completely miss it?"

Pratt laughed. "Those are questions two and three. I promised to answer only one. Come upstairs."

McDonnell was waiting in his office. "What the hell is going on, Pratt?"

Gordon was also there. "What is your clown prince doing with you, Pratt? He's supposed to be on leave."

The jolly mood began to seep from Pratt's face.

"You weren't here, Flash, and I needed to make a quick decision. Ellis knew where Carolyn Tucci lived and was close by. I grabbed him."

McDonnell frowned. "Pratt, can you assure me we're not going to have any problems because you included someone whose brother is involved in this case?"

The detective sat down on one of the chairs facing his boss's desk.

"No problem whatsoever. Mike Master was dead when we got there."

"Did you get her statement?"

"No. We sent her off to hospital. She had a few cuts on her hands and left shoulder."

"Defending herself from her attacker?"

"Maybe."

"What the hell do you mean, Pratt?"

Everyone else's expressions held the same question.

"All will be revealed after the hospital's got her patched up—when she's brought in to give her statement."

McDonnell's phone rang.

"Yes…I figured as much…No, I'm not exactly sure what's going on…I understand that…Yes. I will call you as soon as I have a handle on where we stand…Right. ASAP." He hung up. "That was the press office. The lobby is flooded with media.

They're all demanding to know what's going on." He leveled his gaze at Pratt. "Would you mind telling me just what the hell is going on?"

"I hope to be able to tell you that in a few hours." Pratt stood up wearily. "Now if you'll excuse me, I have to prepare some things for the last act in this little drama. The other two band members are waiting in one of the interview rooms. I need to talk to them."

"Now you're saying the girl is involved in these murders?" Gordon nearly shouted. "Where did you come up with such a stupid theory?"

Pratt stopped in the doorway and smiled. "On Facebook."

CHAPTER TWENTY-TWO

Carolyn Tucci wore a look of abject misery as she was led into the interview room. Pratt and McDonnell were sitting at the far side of the table. In the next room, Gordon, Ellis and Cheevers were looking on from behind a two-way mirror.

"Why did you drag me out of the hospital? Haven't I been through enough today?" she asked, obviously annoyed.

Pratt ignored her questions. "Thank you so much for coming down."

"But I don't want to be here!"

"Just the same, we appreciate you assisting us. I have a few things that need clearing up. Just minor questions, really. May I offer you a coffee or a cold drink? Perhaps a sandwich?"

"I don't want anything. I just want to get out of here."

Pratt said soothingly, "I understand that you've been through a lot."

"Been through a lot? I should be dead. Someone tried to kill me today! How do you think that feels?"

"Why don't you tell me?"

"I don't believe it." She put her head down on the table and moaned, then looked up. "Why don't you just leave me alone?"

"We will, Carolyn, as soon as we straighten out a few things. We came to your apartment and found a person who'd been stabbed to death. You were the only other person there. We have to be certain about what happened. You told us you couldn't remember."

"I still can't. Master came at me with a big-ass knife. The next thing I know, he's dead and you've just broken down my door. I have no idea what happened in between."

"It did look like self-defense."

Tucci sat up straight. "Looked like self-defense? It *was* self-defense. That madman tried to kill me!"

"Did he?"

"Are you saying I made this whole thing up?"

"I'm trying to get to the truth."

McDonnell tapped Pratt on the arm and got to his feet, and they left the room. Pratt followed him to the observation room next door.

"Where are you going with this?" McDonnell asked.

"Yeah," Gordon chimed in. "I'd like to know that too."

McDonnell pointed a finger at him.

"You know what, Flash? Just shut the hell up if you can only make stupid comments."

Pratt looked through the mirror into the next room. Carolyn was slumped back in her chair, eyes shut.

"The two other boys in the band told me some interesting things," he began slowly. "They didn't say anything earlier, probably out of a sense of loyalty. The long and short of it is, Carolyn was playing both Jamie Clark and Mike Master. She's not what she seems."

Pratt went back to the interview room. Sitting at the table across from Carolyn, he waited until she finally looked up. McDonnell slipped in but stayed near the door.

"Carolyn," Pratt said, "I have Fedrano and Blair down the hall. They've been telling me about you and Jamie Clark and Mike Master."

"What did they tell you?" she sneered. "They don't like me. Everything they've said is lies."

"Did you sleep with Mike Master last night?"

"I wouldn't do that to Jamie."

"Even though you tried to sneak out quietly, both of the other band members saw you leave. They also heard you earlier in Master's room."

"All lies!"

"Would you submit to a vaginal swab to prove that?"

She squeezed her eyes shut and took a couple of deep breaths. "Okay. I was with Mike last night."

"The fact is, you've been with him many times, haven't you? Don't bother telling me they're lying. They've signed statements confirming it."

Again a pause. "Yes…"

"Earlier today, I found another knife at The Boom Room. It was attached to the speaker magnet on one of the band's amplifiers."

"So? What does that have to do with me?"

"Quite a great deal. You see, while the knife had been wiped clean of fingerprints, there were a number of other prints and smudges on the speaker magnet." Pratt raised his voice. "None of them were Mike Master's, but they were all from the same person."

Carolyn's eyes were big. "Jamie?"

Pratt shook his head. "No. You. You put that knife there."

"I didn't!"

"Then how did your prints get there?"

"I don't know. I must have touched the magnet on Mike's amp sometime at a rehearsal or something."

"I didn't say it was Mike's amp, so how could you know that?"

"I just assumed—"

Now Pratt's voice was stern. "You put it there on purpose. You needed to get rid of that knife so it wouldn't be found when we searched. You thought it would be undetectable there, and you were almost right. You nearly got away with it."

"Lies! All lies!"

"You stabbed Joseph Lewis like you promised Mike you would. He wanted to take over the band, but to do that, he needed to get rid of Jamie. So you had to make it look as if Jamie had done it. That's why you used the second knife to kill Lewis. If you'd used Jamie's—which you'd taken earlier—you would have wiped off all his prints when you wiped off yours. You needed Jamie's prints on that knife. After Lewis was dead, you carefully stuck Jamie's knife into the wound to get blood on the blade. Then you chucked it under the photocopier. You had to hide the fact there was a second knife."

"You're crazy! Why would I do that? I love Jamie!"

"No, you don't. You latched on to Jamie because you thought he'd become famous. Then you found he didn't have the same fire in his belly that Mike Master had. You said you knew nothing about Mike Master's past, but you knew all about it. Lying with you after sex, he told you his whole story, didn't he?"

"He told me he once killed someone, but I didn't believe him."

"Then, after you'd done just as he'd asked, you found out Master had lied to you. I'll bet it was something like, 'What do you know about managing a band, Carolyn? That's a laugh! I've spoken to Carl Thomson. He's going to be managing Rotten Attitude. He actually knows something about managing a band.' I'll bet that really stung, didn't it? Master had set you up and used you. He was very good at stuff like that."

Carolyn started to speak, then flopped back in her chair, glaring at Pratt.

He continued speaking.

"You had an ace up your sleeve though, didn't you? All you had to do was plant a little bug in Jamie's half brother's ear. Jamie had told you he was a straight-arrow cop. He'd make sure Mike Master got his due. Master's knife was still where you'd hidden it, but then we didn't find it. You'd hidden it too cleverly. So today you took matters into your own hands. You set Master up. You were lying in wait for him at your apartment. You stabbed him with the hunting knife you took from his room last night. Then you made it look like he'd attacked you. All you had to do was wait for us to show up with the idea we were saving you from a psychopath."

Carolyn wouldn't even raise her eyes as she began weeping.

CHAPTER TWENTY-THREE

Hours later, in the police department's favorite bar, Pratt sat with Ellis and McDonnell. He really could have used some sleep, but the bourbon was going down very nicely.

"The thing I don't get is, you told Gordon you came up with the solution by looking at Facebook," McDonnell said. "Everyone knows you can't stand computers, much less operate one."

Pratt clapped Ellis on the back. "It was all with young David's help. And you know what? It wasn't hard at all. I've been wary of computers for no good reason, as it turns out."

"But what did you see on Facebook?"

"Yeah," Ellis chimed in. "I looked at all those pages too. There wasn't anything there that could have led you to Carolyn Tucci. Come on, Mervin," he said, using Pratt's given name for the first time ever. "Spill the beans."

"As I've told you before, David, you can't just look, you have to see."

"Pratt!" said McDonnell. "As your superior officer, I order you to answer my question."

Pratt turned to him. "The Rotten Attitude fan page on Facebook is moderated—if that is the correct word—by our Carolyn. Perhaps it's her ego, but her digital fingerprints are all over it."

"Listen to you." Ellis laughed. "Digital fingerprints, indeed!"

"So what was it you noticed?" McDonnell asked again.

"Simply that Carolyn reported we'd found that first knife a good half hour before we told the media. The date and time of the posting is right there for all to see. Equally telling, there were all her reports about how the band would carry on without its founder and chief songwriter. Master would finally have control of the band—and she did it all for him. She was fawning all over him."

Ellis shook his head, then swallowed the last of his beer. "You told her you knew about Thomson getting the shot at managing the band. Did you actually know that?"

"Sure. That's about the one useful thing Gordon did on this job. Say what you will about him, Gordon knows how to wring a confession out of someone."

McDonnell motioned to the bartender for refills. They'd all regret this the next morning.

"Okay, Pratt, since you're so smart, who was the mastermind? The dead singer or Carolyn Tucci?"

"Based on what Sheriff Warsh told me, I'm pretty sure it was Master pulling the strings. But there's probably no way we'll ever find out. Warsh thinks Master was borderline psychotic. The scary thing was that he was near-genius in intelligence. We all know well those are the worst kind."

Pratt took a sip of his new bourbon.

"Still, he may have met his match in Carolyn Tucci. Whether it was an extreme need for fame or whether she's psychotic too, we'll have to wait to find out. Anyway, knowing all about Master's past, it was a pretty good bet we'd believe he tried to kill her. It came close to working too. It nearly took me too long to realize there might be a second knife."

"And you got Jamie off," Ellis said. "I can't thank you enough. It's interesting…"

"What is?" both older men asked.

"I listened to the CD of the band Carolyn gave me. I never really liked Jamie's kind of music, but I have to admit his songs are, well, pretty good. I found myself liking them. I should play it for you."

McDonnell and Pratt looked at each other in horror.

"No, thanks," Pratt said. "Don't make me regret what I've just done!"

ACKNOWLEDGMENTS

The usual suspects (my wife Vicki and the indomitable Cheryl Freedman) again scanned my deathless prose, found it *not* deathless, but fortunately made suggestions that helped resuscitate every phrase to full health. Anything that's still wrong is my fault, *not* theirs! I was also aided in all things police-oriented by Brent Pilkey who knows about this sort of stuff, nuff said!

RICK BLECHTA has two passions in life: music and writing. A professional musician since age fourteen, he brings his extensive knowledge of that life to his crime fiction. He is the author of nine novels, one of which, *Cemetery of the Nameless*, was shortlisted for the Arthur Ellis Best Novel Award (2005). *The Boom Room* is his second title in the Rapid Reads series, following *Orchestrated Murder* (2012). Rick lives, writes and performs in Toronto, Ontario. For more information, visit www.rickblechta.com.